THE STORY ABOUT PING

BY

MARJORIE FLACK

AND

KURT WIESE

THE VIKING PRESS, NEW YORK

3   4   5   74   73   SBN 670–05041–5

ONCE upon a time there was a beautiful young
duck named Ping. Ping lived with his mother
and his father and two sisters and three brothers
and eleven aunts and seven uncles and forty-two cousins.
Their home was a boat with two wise eyes on the
Yangtze river.

Each morning as the sun rose from the east, Ping and his mother and his father and sisters and brothers and aunts and uncles and his forty-two cousins all marched, one by one, down a little bridge to the shore of the Yangtze river.

All day they would hunt for snails and little fishes and other pleasant things to eat. But in the evening as the

sun set in the west, "La-la-la-la-lei!" would call the Master of the boat.

Quickly Ping and all his many family would come scurrying, quickly they would march, one by one, up over the little bridge and on to the wise-eyed boat which was their home on the Yangtze river.

Ping was always careful, very very careful not to be last, because the last duck to cross over the bridge always got a spank on the back.

But one afternoon as the shadows grew long, Ping did not hear the call because at that moment Ping was wrong side up trying to catch a little fish.

By the time Ping was right side up his mother and his father and his aunts were already marching, one by one, up over the bridge. By the time Ping neared the shore, his uncles and his cousins were marching over, and by the time Ping reached the shore the last of his forty-two cousins had crossed the bridge!

Ping knew he would be the last, the very last duck if he crossed the bridge. Ping did not want to be spanked.

So he hid.

Ping hid behind the grasses, and as the dark came and the pale moon shone in the sky Ping watched the wise-eyed boat slowly sail away down the Yangtze river.

All night long Ping slept near the grasses on the bank of the river with his head tucked under his wing, and when the sun rose up from the east Ping found

he was all alone on the Yangtze river.

There was no father or mother, no sisters or brothers, no aunts or uncles, and no forty-two cousins to go fishing with Ping, so Ping started out to find them, swimming down the yellow waters of the Yangtze river.

As the sun rose higher in the sky, boats came. Big boats and little boats, fishing boats and beggars' boats, house boats and raft boats, and all these boats had eyes to see with, but nowhere could Ping see the wise-eyed boat which was his home.

Then came a boat full of strange dark fishing birds.
Ping saw them diving for fish for their Master. As each
bird brought a fish to his Master he would give it a little
piece of fish for pay.

Closer and closer swooped the fishing birds near Ping. Now Ping could see shining rings around their necks, rings of metal made so tight the birds could never swallow the big fish they were catching.

Swoop, splash, splash, the ringed birds were dashing here and there all about Ping, so down he ducked and

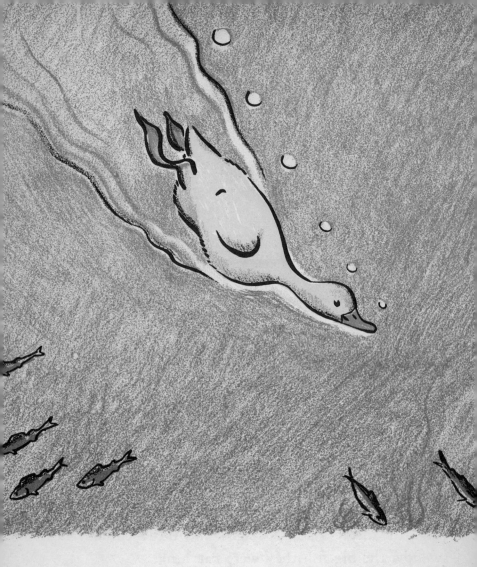

swam under the yellow water of the Yangtze river.
When Ping came up to the top of the water far away

from the fishing birds, he found little crumbs floating,
tender little rice cake crumbs which made a path to a
house boat.

As Ping ate these crumbs, he came nearer and nearer
to the house boat, then——

SPLASH!

There in the water was a Boy! A little boy with a barrel on his back which was tied to a rope from the boat just as all boat boys on the Yangtze river are tied to their boats. In the Boy's hand was a rice cake.

"Oh-owwwwoooo!" cried the little Boy, and up
dashed Ping and snatched at the rice cake.

Quickly the Boy grabbed Ping and held him tight.
"Quack-quack-quack-quack!" cried Ping.
"OH!—Ohh-ooo!" yelled the little Boy.

Ping and the Boy made such a splashing and such a
noise that the Boy's father came running and the Boy's
mother came running and the Boy's sister and brother
came running and they all looked over the edge of the
boat at Ping and the Boy splashing in the water of the
Yangtze river.

Then the Boy's father and mother pulled at the rope which was tied to the barrel on the little Boy's back.

They pulled and they pulled and up came Ping and the

Boy on to the house boat.

"Ah, a duck dinner has come to us!" said the Boy's father.

"I will cook him with rice at sunset tonight," said the Boy's mother.

"NO-NO! My nice duck is too beautiful to eat," cried the Boy.

But down came

a basket all over Ping and he could see no more of the
Boy or the boat or the sky or the beautiful yellow water
of the Yangtze river.

All day long Ping could see only the thin lines of
sun which shone through the cracks in the basket, and
Ping was very sad.

After a long while Ping heard the sound of oars and felt the jerk, jerk, jerk of the boat as it was rowed down the Yangtze river.

Soon the lines of sunshine which came through the cracks of the basket turned rose color, and Ping knew the sun was setting in the west. Ping heard footsteps coming near to him.

The basket was quickly lifted, and the little Boy's hands were holding Ping.

Quickly, quietly, the Boy dropped Ping over the side of the boat and Ping slipped into the water, the beautiful yellow water of the Yangtze river.

Then Ping heard this call, "La-la-la-la-lei!"

Ping looked and there near the bank of the river was
the wise-eyed boat which was Ping's home, and Ping saw
his mother and his father and his aunts, all marching, one
by one, up over the little bridge.

Swiftly Ping turned and swam, paddling toward the
shore. Now Ping could see his uncles marching, one by
one.

Paddle, paddle, Ping hurried toward the shore. Ping
saw his cousins marching, one by one.

Paddle, paddle, Ping neared the shore, but—

As Ping reached the shore the last of Ping's forty-
two cousins marched over the bridge and Ping knew that
he was LATE again!

But up

marched Ping, up over the little bridge and SPANK

came the spank on Ping's back!

Then at last Ping was back with his mother and his father and two sisters and three brothers and eleven aunts and seven uncles and forty-two cousins. Home again on the wise-eyed boat on the Yangtze river.